happy yak

Here are the Ploofers.

They are going to do something very special,
all together.

They have been practising...

They will do it at the same time...

READY, STEADY...

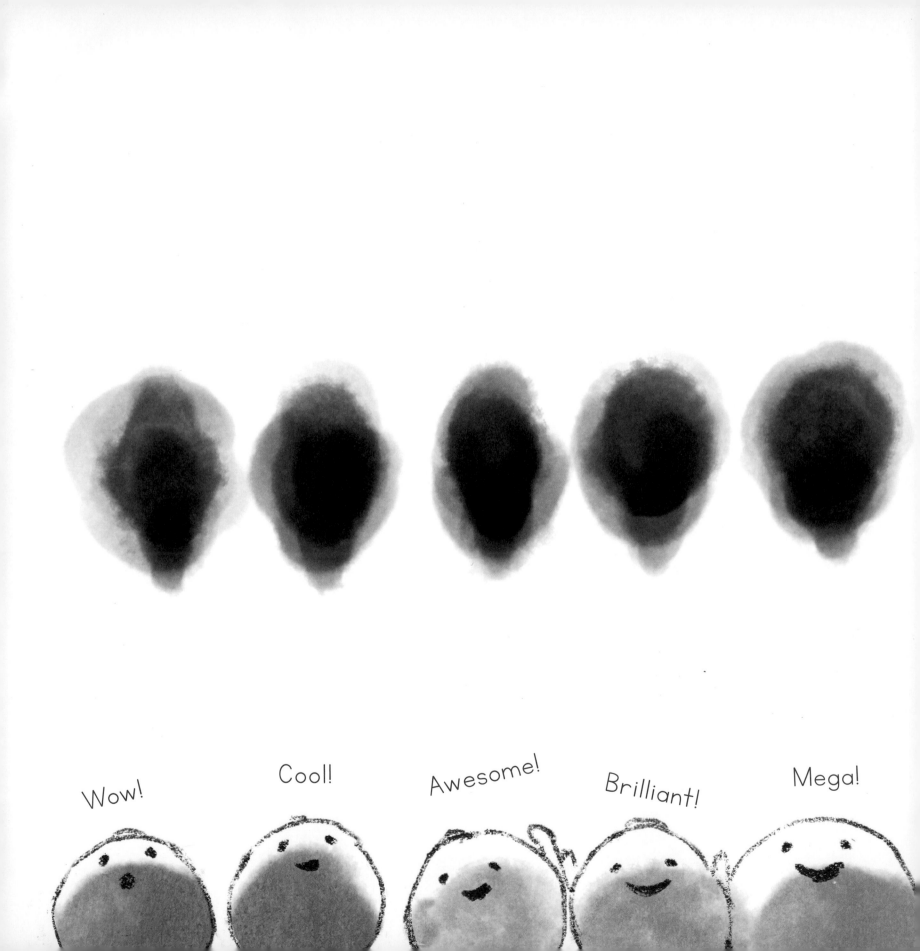

Wow!

Cool!

Awesome!

Brilliant!

Mega!

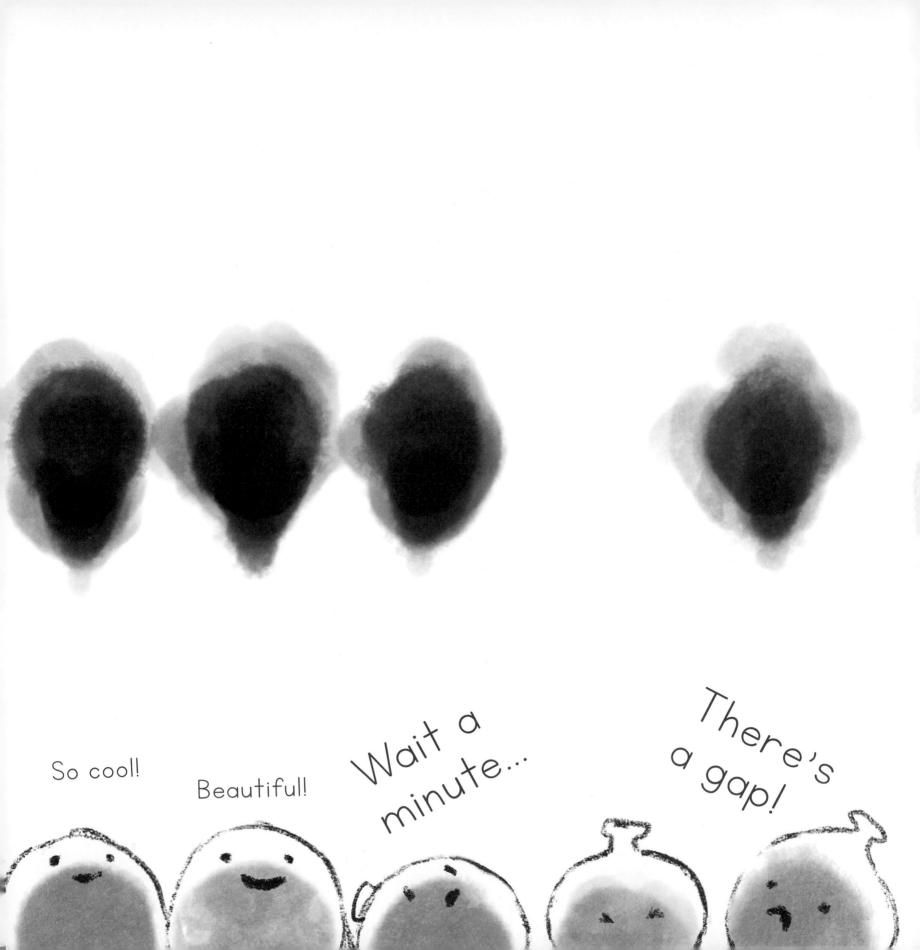

I don't know, but

I LOVE IT!

BUT IT'S DIFFERENT!

Well, it is different!

I don't like it...

It's WEIRD!

Let's go!

They didn't like it.

Why didn't they like it?

WOW!
Did you make that?

It's
beautiful!

Do you think so?

Yes! It's BIG and BRIGHT and
COLOURFUL, and SO DIFFERENT!

Look!

They are quite special...

They REALLY are SPECIAL!

Let's all **SHOOF** like you!

REMDY, STEADY...

For Jodie and Jo

Quarto is the authority on a wide range of topics.

Quarto educates, entertains and enriches the lives of our readers—enthusiasts and lovers of hands-on living.

www.quartoknows.com

This edition published in 2021 by Happy Yak,
an imprint of The Quarto Group.
The Old Brewery, 6 Blundell Street,
London N7 9BH, United Kingdom.
T (0)20 7700 6700 F (0)20 7700 8066
www.quartoknows.com

A catalogue record for this book is available from the British Library.

ISBN: 978 0 7112 4547 1

9 8 7 6 5 4 3 2 1

Manufactured in Guangdong, China CC042021

FSC
www.fsc.org
MIX
Paper from responsible sources
FSC® C008047